To my very dear friend Neil Mountain, with love
S.J-P.

To my mother, Ella Macnaughton
T.M.

Sandy Creek
387 Park Avenue South
New York, NY 10016

SANDY CREEK and the distinctive Sandy Creek logo are trademarks
of Barnes and Noble, Inc.

This 2012 custom edition is published exclusively for Sandy Creek by Parragon Books Ltd.

Published by arrangement with Gullane Children's Books 185 Fleet Street, London, EC4A 2HS

Text © Susie Jenkin-Pearce 2005 Illustrations © Tina Macnaughton 2005

ISBN 978-1-4351-4434-7
Printed and bound in Guangzhou, China
10 9 8 7 6 5 4 3 2 1 Lot
08/11/2012

Pugwug and Little

Sandy Creek
NEW YORK

Pugwug was out slipping, and sliding,
when **BANG**,
he bumped into something **BIG.**

Pugwug just had to know what
all the penguins were looking at.

He **bounced**...   He **flapped**...

He tried **diving** through a tiny gap...

but it was no use.

Eventually, Big Penguin turned around.
On his feet there was something
large and round.

"Pugwug," said Big Penguin,
"meet your new little brother . . . or maybe sister!"

Pugwug was beside himself.
He shrieked with delight.
"Come on, Little,"
he yelled,
"let's play!"

But Little did not seem to want to play.
In fact, Little did **nothing at all**.

Pugwug tried to make Little look more
like a brother . . . or sister!

But he made a bit of a mess.
So Big Penguin had to give Little a wash.

"Come on—let's race!" said Pugwug.

"Or . . . let's play catch!" said Pugwug.

"Maybe not . . ." said Big Penguin gently.

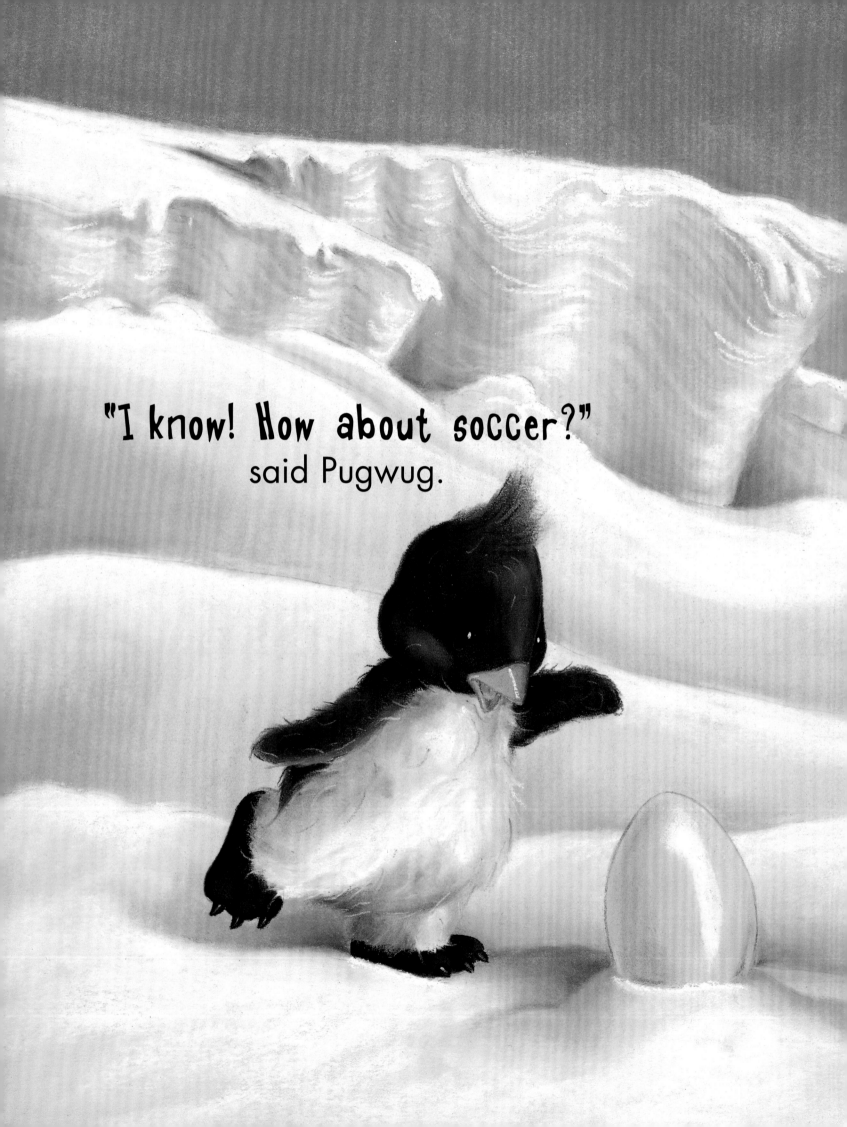

Big Penguin
was exhausted!

Suddenly a shout went up:
"Danger—seal alert! Penguin in trouble!"

"Pugwug," said Big Penguin gravely,
"look after Little. Watch, but don't TOUCH!"
Then Big Penguin flapped away as fast as he could.

Pugwug and Little were all on their own.
Suddenly, Little began to **wobble**...

and **shake** and **rock** and **roll**...

Pugwug didn't
know what to do...

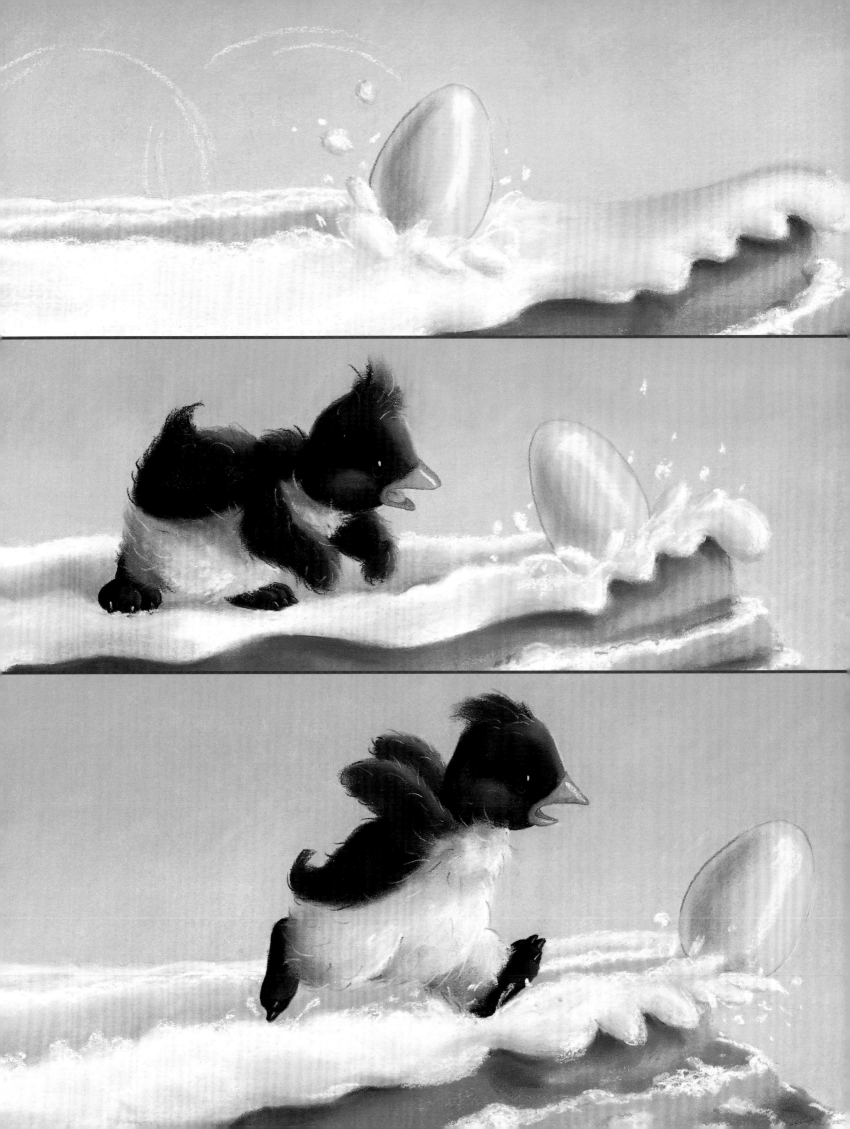

. . . but then he realized **he HAD to touch!**

Pugwug made a **great dive** and clasped Little close to him.

And then...

When Big Penguin returned,
he found Little snuggled against Pugwug.
"Big Penguin," said Pugwug,
"meet my new baby...
sister!"